Yogi Superhero

by Anna Smithers

ISBN: 9781654493363

For my two,
very special Yogi Superheroes
– Wiktoria and Sofia

I am a Yogi Superhero,
filled with love and light.

I spread care, joy and kindness
and make the world nice and bright.

I am a Yogi Superhero,
filled with love and light.
Standing tall like a mountain,
majestic in its might.

With one foot, two feet,
firmly on the ground,
watching the world in stillness,
passing me by around.

I move my legs wide
and lift my arms high,
saying loud to myself:
I am strong, I am brave, I am not shy.

And like a Yogi Warrior
standing strong on the floor,
I notice the quietness
and stillness of my core.

Now I bring the legs together
and stand strong on one foot,
flying high above the trees
and taking the bird's route.
Bending forward with the whole body,
pretending I can fly,
like a yogi superhero soaring to the sky.

I go down on my knees
with hands straight on the ground,
listening to my in and out breaths,
making the quiet sound.
Breathing in - lower my back down
and look in front of me,
noticing what is around,
and everything I can see.

Breathing out -arching my back
and lowering my head to the floor,
stretching my spine like a cat
rubbing against a door.

I lie down on my back
and bring my knees to my chest,
moving my legs up and down,
allowing my back to rest.

Side to side, hugging my knees
and leading with my heels,
noticing everything inside me
and how my mind feels.

I am a Yogi Superhero
filled with love and light.
But sometimes my mind is buzzing
like a million bees in flight.

And I feel all those emotions
of anger, fear and sadness,
and I have no idea
how to convert them to kindness.

So, I sit on the floor
with my finger in front of my mouth,
starting to breathe in through my nose
and out through my mouth,
counting to ten out loud.

The breath touches my finger
and I start to feel calmer,
I feel joy and peace again
and my heart becomes warmer.

And I repeat again —
I am a Yogi Superhero
filled with love and light.

I spread care, joy and kindness
and make the world nice and bright.

Other Yogi Superhero Stories:

Yogi Superhero
Adventures in Nature - Forest

Yogi Superhero
Time to Rest

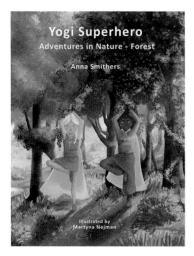

From the Author

Dear Adult - Thank you for reading this book! If you enjoyed it, please consider leaving a review. It would mean the world to me! Thank you.

Hi Children - If you have any ideas for new Yogi Superhero adventures, I would love to hear from you! I also love receiving letters, drawings and pictures. Feel free to email anna@annasmithers.com and I will try my best to email you back!

A. Smithers

Anna Smithers is an author, fully qualified yoga teacher and yoga therapist for children and young adults. She specialises in working with children and people with autism. Anna holds two masters degrees; in Science and Business Management. Her Yogi Superhero Adventures in Nature – Forest won a bronze medal in a children's picture book category in Living Now US Awards 2020.

Martyna Nejman is an illustrator who lives in Warsaw, Poland. She became interested in drawing when she was a teenager, using traditional drawing techniques. Nowadays she mostly uses digital methods. Martyna collaborates with publishers as well as with individual clients. She creates children's illustrations, posters, portraits and book covers. More information on https://martynanejman.wixsite.com/ilustrator-portfolio